InvestiGATORS
Off the Hook

InvestiGATORS

Off the Hook

written and illustrated by

John Patrick Green

with color by **Aaron Polk**

To Steve, Heidi, Amy,
and the rest of the DA crew.

:01
First Second

Drawn on Strathmore Smooth Bristol paper with Staedtler Mars Lumograph H pencils, inked with Sakura Pigma Micron and Staedtler Pigment Liner pens, and digitally colored in Photoshop.

Published by First Second
First Second is an imprint of Roaring Brook Press,
a division of Holtzbrinck Publishing Holdings Limited Partnership
120 Broadway, New York, NY 10271

Library of Congress Control Number: 2020911278

ISBN: 978-1-250-22000-4 (Hardcover)
ISBN: 978-1-250-80169-2 (Special Edition)

First edition, 2021
Edited by Calista Brill, Rachel Stark, and Dave Roman
Cover design by John Patrick Green and Kirk Benshoff
Interior book design by John Patrick Green
Color by Aaron Polk
Printed in China by Toppan Leefung Printing Ltd., Dongguan City, Guangdong Province

10 9 8 7 6 5 4 3 2 1

Chapter 1

Under cover of night...
chugga chugga chugga chugga chugga

...a train speeds along a mountain pass!
Tickets?
Tickets?
chugga chugga chugga chugga chu

Tickets?
And **ALSO** undercover on that train are the...

INVESTIGATORS!
AAAH!

MANGO! Stop narrating! You're gonna blow my cover!

BOOP

Sorry, Brash...

You know how much I like trains. I just got carried away!
Remember, *your* cover is to keep the train running safely...
EMERGENCY BRAKE

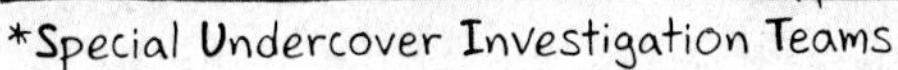
*Special Undercover Investigation Teams

Oh, excuse me, so sorry!
No, no, entirely my fault!

Wait a sec—You're **CRACKERDILE!**

It seems nothing gets past **YOU**, Agent Brash.
That's why I'm going to...
PROPERTY of S.U.I.T.

...RUN THE OTHER WAY!
Mango! Crackerdile is on the train! And he has the stolen S.U.I.T.case!
PROPERTY of S.U

I'll come help!
No, stay there!

Your mission is at the *front* of the train!
But Brash—

Mango, I need you there in case Crackerdile doubles back, or has sabotaged the train, or if—

!
ZAP

Looks like you're beaten. What a *shock*!
If what? Brash?

Brash? BRASH?!

Hmm...

A drone?

Stay at the front...
Stay at the front...
Stay at the front...
PACE
PACE
PACE

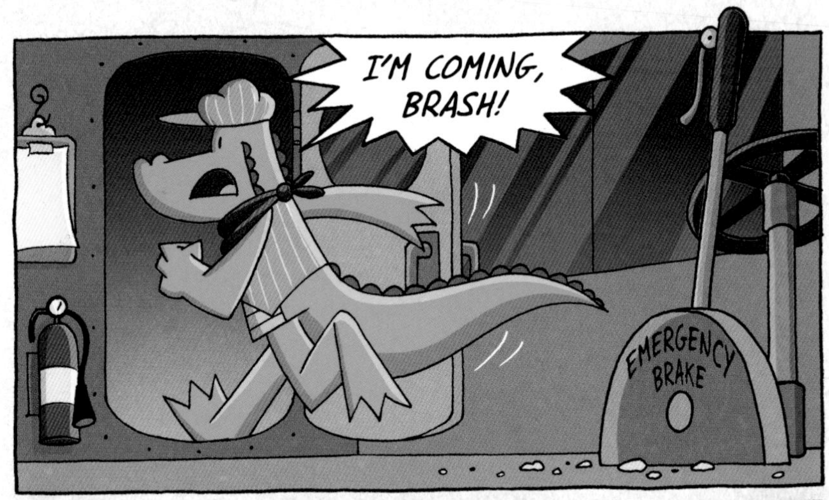
I'M COMING, BRASH!
EMERGENCY BRAKE

Pardon...
Coming through...
Don't mind me...
chugga chugga chugga chugga chu

GASP!

Well, well, well, Agent Mango.
Let Brash go!
I don't think he'd like that.
PROPERTY of S.U.I.T.

You've got two options: Save your partner from falling to his doom...

...or stop this train before it plummets off that bridge!
Beep
DETONATOR

00:01
BOOM!

There's not enough time to do both, so choo-choo-choose wisely!

What do I do?
What do I do?!

Forget about me, Mango! Your mission is at the front of the train!

NO! I won't let you die, Brash!
PROPERTY of S.U.I.T.

PROPERTY of S.U.I.T.
Oops.
DROP

Brash!
AAAAAAA

PROPERTY of S.U.I.T.
LATER, GATOR!

DIVE!
AAAAAA

Mango! Why'd you jump after me? Now you won't be able to stop the train in time!

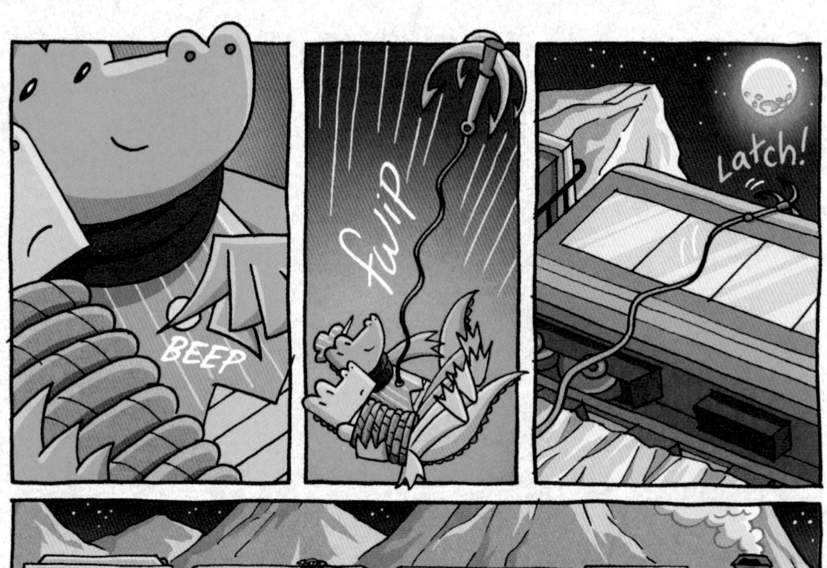
BEEP
fwip
Latch!

ssswwwiiinnnggg!

Just in time!
EMERGENCY BRAKE

YANK!
EMERGENCY BRAKE

SNAP
EMERGENCY BRAKE

Oh, no!

The bread crumbs! Crackerdile must have sabotaged the emergency brake!
EMERGENCY BRAKE

chugga chugga chug—

AAAAAAAAAAAAAAAAAAAAAAAAA

KABOOM!!

AAAAAA—huh?

OW!
smack

BZZT!
SIMULATION FAILED!
EXIT
Darn it!

Chapter 2

Deep inside S.U.I.T. Headquarters...
TRAINING SIMULATOR
RAINING SIMULAT
fssh
tap tap tap

Mango, you've run that training simulation a dozen times and you *still* haven't gotten it right.
It's not fair, Brash! It's a **no-win scenario!**

Even if I let Crackerdile *kill you* and I get to the front of the train *before* he bombs the bridge, the brakes are out, and we all go over the cliff anyway.

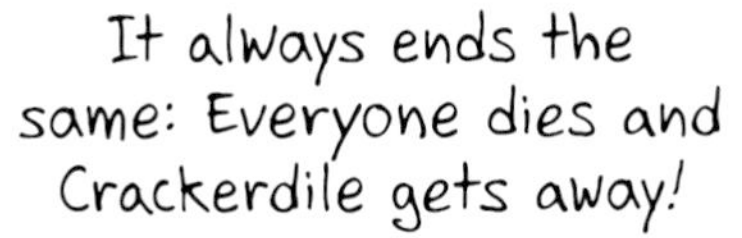
It always ends the same: Everyone dies and Crackerdile gets away!

BRAINING SIMULATOR

Have you tried...*not* saving me ***OR*** stopping the train, but *just* capturing Crackerdile?

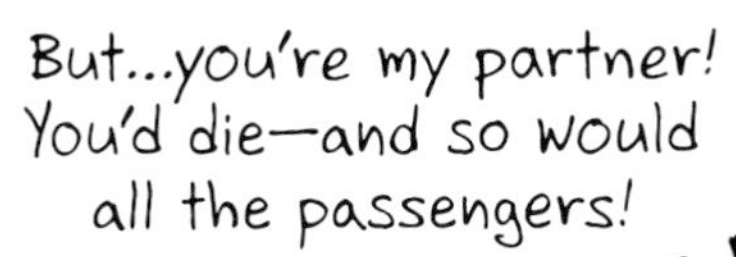
But...you're my partner! You'd die—and so would all the passengers!

True. But you've got to think about the **GREATER GOOD.**

Crackerdile is a threat to **thousands,** maybe **MILLIONS** of people—maybe even the **WHOLE WORLD!** No matter what happens to me or the people on that train, if he *gets away,* the mission is a *failure!*
BRAINING SIMULATOR
REIGNING SIMULATOR

What do you mean he's a threat to thousands? Last time we saw him he was a **pile of mush** that probably got washed out to sea. I don't even know why I'm training to stop him.

You're right. Crackerdile ***ISN'T*** a threat anymore. But if you can't beat ***him,*** what if there's a villain even ***MORE*** dangerous than a former-agent-turned-radioactive-saltine-cracker?

Sometimes there is no GOOD choice. But you still have to make A choice.
Yeah, I guess you're right. For the GREATER GOOD.
SI
Who comes up with these scenarios, anyway?
STAINING SI
SIMULATOR
That would be me.
STAINING SI
AAAH!

Mango, you know **Cilantro**. You and she were **junior agents** around the same time, right?
Yup!
Oh, I...don't recall seeing you. I'm so sorry.
Don't be! Not seeing me is the whole point. I'm a ***chameleon!***
I can change my skin patterns and colors to blend in with my surroundings.

*Computerized Ocular Remote Butler

HA HA! I'm kidding. I'm a giant unblinking eyeball. I see *everything!*

EVERYTHING.

Mango, this says we need to head to the Science Factory, ASAP! It's about the **Bill Plungerman** case!

You mean the case of the missing plumber whose *arm* was combined with a *snake,* giving him grappling hook powers?
We've been trying everything to find him.

*Apparel Research and Manufacturing...Service? Section? Something?

Why always vests? Why not something like... a trench coat? Trench coats are way cool... So mysterious...

You can never tell if someone's a GOOD GUY or a BAD GUY if they're in a trench coat!

We're GOOD GUYS no matter what we wear, Mango...

But we are In-VEST-igators, not In-TRENCH COAT-igators. That doesn't even make sense!

Chapter 3

That morning in the city...

MOOVERS
from COWST to COWST

ziiiippp!

LATCH!

WOOOSH
MOOVERS
from COWST to COWST
WOOOSH
Uh...
WOOOSH

Hey, wasn't there a...

WOOOSH
Yo, Vinny!

Is it me, or do we have less stuff than we did a minute ago?
Heh heh heh!
MOOVERS
from COWST to COWST

SLAM!

Welcome back, **Hookline** and **Slinker**...

...my favorite (and only) member— uh, *members?*—of my evil team,
T.A.I.L.BLAZERS!
Our mission: the Total Annihilation of Idiot Law-doers!

PLOP!
Now, let's take a look at your latest haul...

A lamp? Not sure how it fit in that sack, but okay...

A VCR? Small potatoes! Scented candles? Useless!

A microwave? You can't bake bread in a microwave! Even if you could, it wouldn't taste any good!

And who knows what kind of effect microwaves would have on the **radioactive waste** that courses through my veins...if I even *have* veins...

Bah! None of this junk will help me, **CRACKERDILE**, be restored from this bucket of dough back to my crispy, crackery condition.

rub rub
Not that that crumby carcass was ever all it was cracked up to be.

Before I was cracker dough, I was a cracker. Before *that,* I was a crocodile...who fell into cracker dough...and before *THAT...*
...I was an agent of S.U.I.T. named Daryl...
...and my pa tner,
Agen Bras

I'm BILL PLUNGERMAN, ACE PLUMBER!
This tool is a DRAIN SNAKE. I've named mine Slinker!
SCIEN
FACTO
Bill
Bill
It's a ROBOT GHOST!!
Bill
COMBINE
M-MY ARM!!
HEY!
Are you even listening?
Bill

I'm trying to tell you my **origin story!** *SHEESH!*
Wh-Where am I?
Where? Oh, hmm... Now that you mention it, this vacant lot really doesn't make the best base of operations.
I'll certainly want a nicer place for all my stuff!
HYPNOTIZE!

And if I expect people to join my team, I better have a base that's...grand... EPIC!
Grand... epic... Yesssss...
Well, I'm glad you agree, Hookline and Slinker.
We can fix my doughy disposition later. Now, let's find T.A.I.L.Blazers a new secret lair!!

Chapter 4

I've gotta admit, it's nice to find someone in a predicament similar to my own.
CLOSED

Me, a villanous bucket of unbaked batter. You, a monstrous, plumber-tailed snake. Both of us on a quest for revenge!

I assume! Correct me if I'm wrong, but revenge is a common motivation for villains and monsters.

Hey, what's this? The abandoned opera house! That's both grand AND epic! Hmm... Looks like it's seen better days, but it may have potential for a secret lair.
CLOSED

Krak!
I remember seeing this on the news!

All this damage is from a rocket that launched under the stage.

Look! There's a **rocket base** in the **basement**!
A **ROCKET BASEMENT**!

Check out all the scientific equipment!

We just need a scientist or two to get it working and—

ACK!
Ants!

Guess we'll need an exterminator, too. Well, at least—
Drip

Oh, no! RAIN?

flrp
What the—

PIGEONS?!
splorp

Gah! Nasty! Shoo! SHOO!!

This place is definitely a *fixer-upper*. You may be a plumber, but we'll need a ***lot*** more help—like a bunch of construction workers to repair that roof.

Pigeon poop is one thing, but if we find a way to rebake me **back** into a cracker, I certainly can't risk getting rained on!
flrp
CLOSED

Chapter 5

Back at S.U.I.T. HQ...

Sven! The InvestiGators are here!

Sven?

A.R.M.S.

APPAREL RESEARCH and MANUFACTUR

*Very Exciting Spy Technology

Sven, doesn't the T in V.E.S.T. stand for "technology"?
Hee hee! You just said "technology technology"!
Oh...

I, uh, MEANT to say it! Because these V.E.S.T.s are TWICE as technologically advanced!

Um, Sven? This looks just like my current V.E.S.T.
Am I missing something?

Indeed you are, Brash! Previously you needed a different V.E.S.T. for each new undercover job. But now...

BOOP

COOL! I wanna try it out!
Be my guest!

Toss

Button
Button

Look, Brash! I'm a TRAIN ENGINEER!

What else can I be?
Beep

LUMBERJACK!
Bip

REFEREE!
Bop

CROSSING GUARD!
Boop

New camouflage nanotech can change these V.E.S.T.s' patterns and colors to suit **any disguise** you need to blend in during your investigations.
SPORTBALLER!

Oh, WOW! You finally used my design for chameleon V.E.S.T.s!
Cilantro!
BEP
Have you been there this whole time?
I *knew* my ideas were good enough for the A.R.M.S. Division!
shake-a shake-a
Er...
But...
Thanks, Mr. Septapus!
Check this out, Cilantro!
BEEP

With a press of his V.E.S.T., Mango's ready for the ocean!
HA! I'm gonna hit the beach!

Cilantro's idea should earn her a promotion!
Now I'm a fancy waiter!
Well, I can't wait—
Boop
WAIT! WAIT!! Stop the montage!

I'm sorry, Cilantro, but I didn't get the idea from you. Yes, you're a chameleon, but octopuses can change their color and texture, too.
Bip

I've been perfecting this technology for as long as I can remember.
But...but...

I thought the plural of *octopus* was *octopi*...?
Mmm, pie.
blurp

InvestiGators! Where are you on the Bill Plungerman case?
vvrp
C-ORB gave you that file **25 pages ago!** You should be at the Science Factory by now!

Wait—you're actually wearing *my* new V.E.S.T., Mango. That's the color brown that *I* always wear.

Just put on the other one.

Chapter 6

There! Head into that trailer.

Hashtag dis... Hashtag dat...
WHAM
CONSTRUCTION MAN!

Dat's **FOREman.** What can I do youse for?
I'd like to hire your crew for a quick fix-'em-up job.

Youse got any *dough* for dis job?

Why, *YES!* I'm an entire **BUCKET of DOUGH!**

No, I mean how you gonna *pay* for it? ***Show me da money!***
MONEY?!

Come back when you got some cash!
FINE! I'll be back. Let's go, Hookline.

I meet da strangest peoples on dis job.

Eh, at least my followers like it! #DoughBucket #AngryDough #NoMoney #TrenchCoat
tap
tap
tap

Time to make a withdrawal.
$
BANK

I'll do the talking. We don't want to freak anyone out.
NEXT!

How can I help you?
HAND OVER THE DOUGH!

Uh...
What? NO, not ME!

I meant for *HER* to hand over the *MONEY*!
What **is** this?

Heh heh. Sorry, lady. We're a little new at this.
AHEM
Put the MONEY in the BUCKET.
Um... Okayyy?

kaChing!

Yep. Yeah. Ooh, just like that.

And now, you hand the dough—me AND the money—back over.

And that's it! **BYEEEE!**
Thanksssssssssss!

HA HA! Like giving candy to a baby!
Which is even easier than **taking** candy from a baby!

Uh... What just happened?

blink

blink
blink

WE WERE ROBBED!

SILENT ALARM
Beep!

Chapter 7

Meanwhile...
SCIENCE FACTORY

Ah, Mango and Brash! Welcome back to the Science Factory.
WELCOME to the WORLD of SCIENCE!

Thanks, Doc! It's nice to be here when you're not in the middle of a **science accident**!
Give it time. This is only page 54!

You two remember our serpentologist, Dr. Morrow.
Hello again!
It was *MY* snake that got kidnapped by that plumber Bill Plungerman!
Now, now, Tom. It's possible it was the *plumber* who was kidnapped by your *snake!*
Hmm, true. Snakes **can** be very persuasive.
Does it matter who kidnapped who? The snake's and plumber's bodies were **physically combined** in the last science accident. *One* can't go anywhere without the *other.*

Yes, their bodies were combined. But now their *one body* has *TWO HEADS!* And as the **Head Scientist,** I can tell you that two heads aren't always better than one!
Two heads means two ***BRAINS***, and it's my guess that the brain of the snake and the brain of the plumber are fighting for control over their combined body.

That must be what's made Bill Plungerman so hard to find. Who could predict what a snake brain might do with a plumber body?

I've discovered another wrench in the works. Well, not a *wrench*, but a different tool—

The plumber's **DRAIN SNAKE TOOL!**
That's right. Bill was here to unclog a drain. But *tools* don't have *brains*, Doc.

I saw on security footage from the incident that the snake was wrapped around the tool *and* the plumber's arm at the moment they all got combined.
That tool must be how the snake-arm got grappling hook powers!

With power like that, the snake and/or plumber might not **want** to be found!
OR cured! And uncombining their bodies and minds won't be easy. There's a huge risk of the plumber getting the snake's mind or vice versa.
And one of them could still be combined with the drain snake tool!

But if I can invent a device that can hold both of their minds, we could extract their consciousnesses before we uncombine their bodies—and make sure the right mind winds up in the right body afterward!
Well, first we need to find this plumber-snake combo. Right, Mango?
Mango?

Look, Brash! I'm a SCIENTIST, just like this giant chicken!
Yo.
blurp

Mang⋚KSH⋛ and Bra⋚KSH⋛!
The downtow⋚KSH⋛ bank has been ⋚KSH⋛ robbed!
vvZzrp

Put the Bill Plun⋚KSH⋛ case on ⋚KSH⋛ for ⋚KSH⋛, but keep your ⋚KSH⋛ for ⋚KSH⋛. The robber⋚KSH⋛ could be con⋚KSH⋛ or ⋚KSH⋛side job.

Is your V.E.S.T. glitchy?
Sven did say these are prototypes.
tap tap

Go under≷KSH≷er as INVESTMENT BANKERS and ge≷KSH≷ to the botto≷KSH≷ of it!
Copy that!

This is the perfect opportunity to field test these V.E.S.T.s!
Beep
Boop

Aw, this outfit is BORING. InvestigaBankers just wear gray suits.

You mean "investment bankers."
That's what I said, InvestigaBankers.
Invest*ment* bankers.
Investiga-Bankers.

Ah, forget it. We need to get to the bank PRONTO!
My name's MANGO.
"Pronto" means QUICKLY!

Doctor, where's the restroom?

Oh, right! You Gators get around town by flushing yourselves into the sewers.

Right in here!

Whoa, Doc, this looks like something straight out of *science fiction!*
This is the *Toilet of the Future*™! It was made with **science FACT!**
Don't worry, it's perfectly safe.
Hold on to your butts!
CRANK
FLOOOOOOSH!
blup

Chapter Aiden—I MEAN—8

Now repair the roof on my **secret lair**—*I MEAN*— the **opera house!**
Yeah, okays. I can schedule your job in, uh...six months.
scroll
scroll
scroll
WHADDYA MEAN YOU'LL DO THE JOB IN SIX MONTHS?!
No, no. I didn't say dat.
I said I can ***schedule*** da job in six months.
Meaning, in half a year I can looks at my *calendar*, and *DEN* I can find a time dat my crew can do your job.
So youse probably lookin' at a **whole year** from now 'fore we can get to it.

A YEAR?!!

Aw, dis is too funny! #AngryDoughBucket I gotta get a picture of youse. *Heh heh!*

flash
HISS
!

MY EYES!
Whuh—

Where am I...?
HISSS!

HYPNOTIZE!

I don't believe it!

You spilled DOUGH all over my desk!
HEY!

Dat's it, I'm callin' da cops!
HISSSSSS!

I mean...

I'm gonna tell my crew to fix da opera house...
nod

Wait a minute—you can **HYPNOTIZE** people?

Why'd we need to rob that bank if you coulda just hypnotized this guy in the first place?!
shrug

ATTENTION, CREW! Drop what you're doing and go repair da opera house!

Whatever you say, boss!
DROP
DROP

But wait... No one's going to want to join a team led by a *soft pile of mush.* I need to pull myself together...make something outta myself. I've gotta get TOUGH! **BULK UP!**

Chapter 9

$
BANK

Thanks, ma'am. We'll see what we can dough. I mean, see what we can **do**.
EMPLOYEES ONLY

I—I need to freshen up after all this excitement!
EMPLOYEES ONLY

OH! Excuse me! You, uh, may want to give it a minute in there, if you know what I mean.

Um, thanks for the warning...?
EMPLOYEE ONLY

OH! Excuse me! You, uh—
GEEZ!

First the robbery, now I've got déjà vu!
Déjà vu?
Oh, that was just my fellow Investiga—uh... banker.

PLOYEES ONLY
You mean, **INVESTMENT** banker.
BLOOP

So, what happened during the robbery?
You can tell us. We're *professionals.*

Well, since you're both investment bankers... A guy showed up with a bucket of dough and demanded *MORE* dough!
By "dough" you mean money? So he had money and wanted *more* money?
siiip

He had **dough** and he wanted **money**. He told me to put the **money** in the bucket of **dough**!
Riiiiight, okay. And you put the **dough** in the bucket he had for the **money**?

GASP! BRASH! You know who likes to rob banks and disguise himself with big coats?!

HOUDINO, THE DINOSAUR ESCAPE ARTIST!

But Mango, Houdino's in the S.U.I.T. Maximum Security Prison.
Not if he BROKE OUT!

Hmm, true. Okay, I'll call the **prison gourd.**

Don't you mean prison *GUARD?*
I meant what I said.

RING
RING

CELLBLOCK 4
You've reached the **PRISON GOURD! Butternut Magee** speaking.

Yes, I'd like to know if **Houdino** is still in his cell?
Okay, hold on...

YO, HOUDINO! YOU STILL IN THERE?

Why? Who's asking?

He wants to know who's asking.

It's Mango! Hi, Houdino! How's the food in—
BEEP

Why'd you hang up?
Mango, if he's in prison, then he's **not** the guy in the trench coat!
Oh, right.

click
Well?
Sorry, man, they hung up!

Hmmm...

That was a dead end.

Why are investment bankers calling prisoners?
Oh! Er, we were just, uh...

Okay, here's the truth: As investment bankers, which we are, we meet a lot of criminals in our line of work, which is investment banking, and—
MANGO!

What?

HA HA! Speaking of criminals, is there anything else you can remember about this guy in the trench coat? You know, for, uh, investment banking purposes?
Yeah, before the funny one brought up dinosaurs, I was going to say that he had a snake for an arm.

THE SNAKE-ARMED MAN!
Was this snake-arm attached to a plumber by any chance?

Uh, I really couldn't tell.
Hmm, then there's no way to be certain *THIS* is the same snake-armed man we're looking for.

Mango, how many snake-armed men do you think there are?!

OF COURSE this is the one we're looking for.

Shouldn't we get back to work? I'm pretty sure our breaks are over by now.
Yes, right! Back to business! And there's no place investment bankers do ***business*** better than in the ***bathroom!***
C'mon, Mango!

Where do you two think you're going?
Oh, we were—
It's time for the BOARD MEETING with our accountants to figure out what to do about the stolen money. It's mandatory for all investment bankers!
Well, you see—
You ARE investment bankers, aren't you?
Um, yes, but...but...
BOARDROOM
NO BUTS!
Unless it's your butts getting into that boardroom!

Chapter 10

Down there! THE **MAW**!

DING
Welcome to the Mother of All Waffles, can I take your order?
BOOM CHICKEN WA-WAFFLES
DRUMBELLS
HOW MUCH CAN YOU BENCH?

SLINKER! Hypnotize this adolescent!
Uh...

Would you like to try our famous Wafflenator?

Or the Cinnamon Chix, our cinnamon-dusted drumstick dessert?

Or our latest item: WUGGETS.
Waffle-flavored chicken nuggets?
?
Huh. I guess mind tricks don't work on teenagers.
ANYWAY, make me a waffle!
What size?
BIG! Like the one outside!
Sir, we only serve small and medium waffles, to discourage overeating.
That just means the MEDIUM waffle is the BIG waffle!
BAH! Whatever!
Make me a MEDIUM WAFFLE!

Okay.
BOOP

Here you are, sir! One medium waffle!
!

NO, you fools! Make *ME* a *WAFFLE!* I want to **BE** a **WAFFLE!**
Ooooohhh... Would you like to be one of our novelty shapes?

Ooh! I didn't think about that. Do you have...a *star* shape? Or maybe... a *dinosaur?*

No, we have... square...or... round.

WHAT? Neither of those shapes are **NOVEL!** Ugh, *fine,* I've already been a ***square*** cracker, so make me into **ONE MEDIUM ROUND WAFFLE!**
Okeydokey!

GOOD! NOW, HAND OVER THE DOUGH!

WUMP

No, not the **MONEY!** This time I mean hand ***ME*** over!

YOINK!

TSSSSSS
OOH! Steamy!

SPLAT
fsshhshh
YEOWCH!

tic
tic
tic tic

DING!

PPSSH!

AHA! I feel...crisp! Powerful!

Or should I say... POWAFFLE!

I, Crackerdile, have been reborn as... WAFFLEDILE!
HA HA!
Revenge will be a dish best served—
SSSsssmile!

Everyone say #SnakeArm selfie!
clik
What the—?! STOP THAT!

Aw, he's so adorable! I'm gonna 'gram him!
clik
I'm no *graham* cracker! I'm no cracker at all, anymore! I'm **WAFFLEDILE!**

Hookline and Slinker! Stop *social-media-izing!* We're trying to keep a low profile! ***ARGH!***
clik

Chapter 11

...and at *THIS* point, we'll be *bankrupt!*
Ugh, when will this end?

Do you have something to share with the rest of the room?
YEAH! This meeting is **BORING!**

All we're doing is staring at charts and drinking bad coffee!

Can't *something* be done to liven it up?
I KNOW! A ***MONTAGE!***

Bankers really like to make charts of money!
I see nothing wrong with that.
But you can't have a pie chart without pie!

Terrible coffee makes their farts smell funny!
Pee-yew!
Funny strange, or funny ha ha?
POOT
This is why I drink tea.

There's nothing duller than talking finance!
Dull is good. Sharp things are dangerous!
Yeah, like your teeth and his wit!

So instead get up on the table and dance!
Come on! There could even be balloons!
The only tables I get on are multiplication tables!
PFFF

Well? What do you think?
NO! You're *supposed* to be bored!

That's what makes it a **BOARD MEETING!**
plop

Mango?
Bleep
Blurp

BRASH! I'm getting hits on the #SnakeArm hashtag!

The snake-armed man was spotted at the **Mother of All Waffles** down the street!
Then we gotta run!

Sorry, there's an, uh, **INVESTMENT EMERGENCY** at the **MAW!**

We're finally on that snake's tail!
Technically that snake no longer *has* a tail, unless we count the plumber!
flbrbrlfrblr
Hey! This meeting isn't over!

Boy, those investment bankers sure were weird!
You're tellin' me!
flbrfr
bap

They weren't even wearing tiny hats!

I keep my lunch under mine!

Moments later, a few blocks away from the bank...
We heard about the snake-armed man demanding waffles! Where is he?
This is MAD.
Yeah, it sounds pretty wild, right?
No, sir, *THIS* is **MAD.** **Mother of All *DONUTS.***

You want the **MAW,** **Mother of All *WAFFLES,*** across the street.
Oh.
BOOM CHOCO DO-DONUTS
DUM JELLS
HOW MUCH CAN YOU BENCH?

MOTHER of ALL DONUTS
MAD
MOTHER of ALL WAFFLES
MAW

EXIT
Stop taking pictures! We've gotta get out of here before—

EXIT
BILL PLUNGERMAN!
STOP RIGHT THERE!

I can't take them on yet. I may have *kicked the bucket*, so to speak, but now I'm just a medium-sized waffle!

I need to be BIGGER, like the waffle on the roof!

That gives me an idea!

DRIVE-
THRU
ROUND
BACK

Bill... Robbing that bank was obviously a cry for help. If you come with us, we will find a cure for you and your arm.
Bill?

Hissssssss name isss HOOKLINE...
...and SSSSSLINKER!

SHATTER

It seems the Head Scientist was right that the two brains are fighting for control.
Clearly, the **snake** is doing all the thinking!
And it's thinking **BAD THOUGHTS!**

STOP
MOTHER of ALL WAFFLES
cronch
MAW
DRIVE-THRU ROUND BACK

How are we going to stop it?

STOP

STOP
Wham
Wham
Wham
C'mon, V.E.S.T.!
Beep
Beep
Beep
OW STOP!
OW STOP!
OW STOP!

Uh...
ZiP
ZiP

CLOBBER!

That wasn't what I had in mind, but it did the trick.
We need better cover!
Beep
I know! A **SMOKE SCREEN!**
PSSH
COUGH That's *HACK* too much!
It won't *CHOKE* turn off!
COUGH! *COUGH!*
Beep Beep Beep
PPSSSHHSHSSH
EXIT
DING
Hookline and Slinker are *COUGH* getting away!
Go *HACK* after them, Mango!
Pssh

MOTHER of ALL WAFFLES
MAW
DRIVE-THRU 'ROUND BACK

Latch!

Beep!
zip
zip

clamp

You...won't...get... AWAY!
rrrrrrrr...

COUGH!
HACK!
COUGH!
Ppsshh

Darn prototype V.E.S.T.! Finally!
POOF

heh heh heh
TWIST
TWIST

Wobble

Tap

RRRNNK-
Huh?
MAW

Oh, no! BRASH!

C'mon, c'mon, c'mon!
beep
beep
beep
beep

fwump
zip
Figures.

What do I do? What do I do?!

release

YANK!
WHAM

DRAT! That was gonna *smash Brash!*

Come on, **H&S**... *AWAY!*
SWOOP

MANGO!
You let Hookline and Slinker get away!

Brash, that ***waffle*** was going to turn you into a ***PANCAKE!*** I couldn't let that happen to my partner!
Didn't you learn **anything** from that training simulation?

Are you *mad* that I saved you?
I'm not mad, just...*disappointed.* Stopping the **bad guy** is the mission, not saving your partner.

You mean like how ***YOU*** didn't save your partner **Daryl** from falling into *radioactive saltine dough* and turning into **Crackerdile?**
Excuse me for not wanting my partner to presumably ***die*** only to come back flattened and looking for ***revenge!***

I—I'm sorry, Brash... That was a low blow.
No, Mango. You're right.

Sometimes looking out for your partner *is* the mission.

After all, I've had to look out for *you*, since you're always one step away from blowing our cover. *AND* I've had to keep a lookout for Daryl ever since he became evil.

Well... I guess I don't have to look out for **THAT** partner anymore, since he's gone forever.
Brash—

Being a secret agent isn't easy, Mango. I've had to make a lot of tough decisions for the **Greater Good.** You will, too.

MOTHER of ALL WAFFLES
Wh-Where are you going?
MAW
DRIVE-THRU ROLLOUD BACK

I'm going inside to see if the employees can tell me why Hookline and Slinker had such a craving for waffles that they had to rob a bank.

Plus, that giant waffle shouldn't have fallen over. Something's not adding up, and it's my mission to find out what.

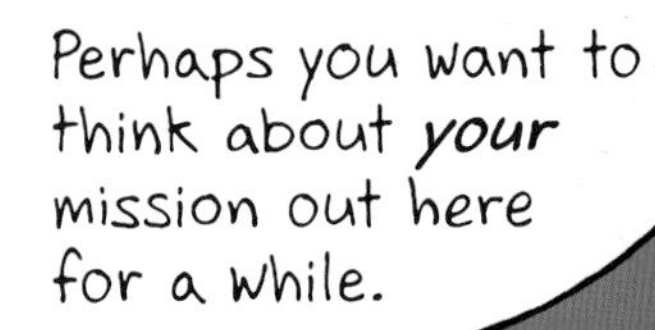

Perhaps you want to think about ***your*** mission out here for a while.
MAW

Another hashtag alert...!
Bleep
Blurp

FANTASTICFOREMAN
Dreamt a guy with a #snakearm made me tell my construction crew to repair the opera house!
Construction crew...? The opera house?! We gotta get over there!

But...
MAW

Hmm...

zip
zip
zip
BOOP

Brash's mission is in there... My mission is out here!
MAW

Chapter 12

That certainly was exciting!

I *love* a good action scene!

But at this size, I'm no match for the **InvestiGators.**

Hookline and Slinker, go back to the opera house and make sure the construction workers—
HOLD ON...

And maybe have them do something about the ants. And tell 'em not to touch any of my stuff!

In the meantime, *I've* got to figure out a way to get ***BIG...***
I could...find a gym? Work out? Pump iron? Take some vitamins? GMOs? Bovine growth hormone?
Make a wish at a carnival game down on the boardwalk?
Nah. Those all sound like **work!**
If only there was an effortless solution to my dilemma...
FA
AHA! The **SCIENCE FACTORY!** They've got plenty of solutions in there!
Especially in the chemistry aisle!
SCIENCE FACTORY

SCIENCE
FACTORY

Sneeak

WELCOME to the WORLD of SCIENCE!

There's *got* to be someone or something in this place that can **EMBIGGEN** me...

WHOA!

That's the biggest chicken I've ever seen!

Of course, at *this* size, ***everything*** looks bigger than I've ever seen!

But as a **crocodile** who turned into a **cracker** who turned into a **waffle**, I've got a little experience with things that are *abnormal*!

He's **GOT** to know some science that will make me bigger.
SIP

DOINK

BUCK BUCK!

Did someone just say "buck buck" at me?
Down here!

Hey, it's a little waffle dude!

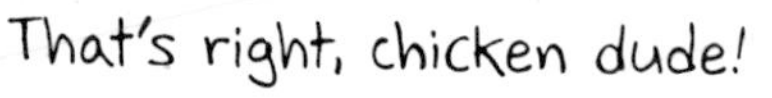
That's right, chicken dude!

That's Chicken Doodledoo to you, dude. DOCTOR Doodledoo.

A doctor, eh? Well I hope you're a doctor...

...of SCIENCE!
TOSS
Lasso!

You're coming with me, you *fowl beast!*
SQUAWK
Leap

SQUAWK!
You're gonna invent a way to make *me* as big as *you!*

GIDDY UP!
HA HA! I feel like a cowboy!

HEY! I'm the only Doctor Cowboy 'round these parts!

STOP! Somebody call security!
You ARE security!
NOW LEAVING the WORLD of SCIENCE!
SQUAWK!

SCIENCE FACTORY

Huh. Chicken and waffles. What will these scientists cook up next?

We got a CODE NO YOLK! Repeat, this is NO YOLK!

Chapter 13

Back at the MAW...
MOTHER of ALL DONUTS
MAD
MAW
DRIVE-THRU 'ROUND BACK

What a mess. Well, at least we recovered the stolen money...

AHEM!
Oh, uh...

I was just making sure it was all there!
Right...
shove

Now, does anyone know why the snake-armed man came into the MAW?

He wanted us to make him a waffle.

So he was just buying waffles with the money he stole from the bank?
No, we made the *DOUGH* into a waffle.
The *dough?* You mean you made waffles out of the *money?*

Not "money" dough. He had a bucket of ***actual*** dough! Like baking dough.

Bucket. Of. Dough.
Yep.

Was it...**CRACKER** dough?!
I dunno, he just said to make him into a waffle! We made him into one of our novelty shapes.

Novelty shape? Like a *star*? Or a *dinosaur*?
No, no, the shape was...uh...um...
Oh, wait! I got a picture of him!

Hold on...nope...nope... Not that one...
Scroll
Scroll
Scroll
Scroll

Here we go! He's *ROUND!*

300 likes

CRACKERDILE!

Cracker? No, that's a WAFFLE.

WAFFLEDILE!

MOTHER of ALL WAFFLES
MANGO!
MANGO!
MAW

Mango? Where could he be?

I've got to warn him that **Crackerdile** is back! And he's a ***WAFFLE!***

Wait! I can reach him on my V.E.S.T.!
Beep

Mango? MANGO?
ksh
ksh
Beep Beep

DRAT! Still on the fritz!

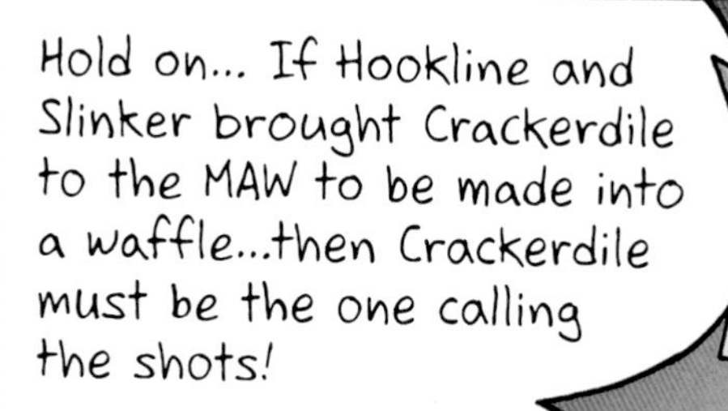
Hold on... If Hookline and Slinker brought Crackerdile to the MAW to be made into a waffle...then Crackerdile must be the one calling the shots!
HE'S the mastermind behind the bank robbery!

THAT'S what the bank teller meant by "bucket of dough"! How could I be so dense?

Smack

Crackerdile couldn't have needed ***ALL*** that money to get *waffle-ized*... So what was it for?
MAW

I should head back to the bank in case I missed any clues.
MAD
MAW

And hopefully that's where Mango went as well!
MAD

Man! That **investment banker** sure is in a hurry!

All units, we have a **BOLO** for a chicken and waffle! Repeat, **Be On the Look Out** for a chicken and waffle!

CHICKEN AND WAFFLES?! I know just where to go!
WOOP WOOP
VROOM
MOTHER of ALL DONUTS
MAD
MOTHER of ALL WAFFLES
MAW
WOOP WOOP
SCREEEEEEEEEEEEECH!!

Yeah, I'd like a *Wafflenator* with a wing, thigh, and extra syrup!
MAW DRIVE-THRU

What?

Chapter 14

CLOSED
Yeah, this place *does* need work.

But what would a snake-armed plumber want with an opera house?
Are these repairs what Hookline and Slinker robbed that bank for?

Gonna be tough paying these construction workers since they left the money at the MAW!

Nothing suspicious so far...
Crunch!

Oh! Well, *THIS* is certainly a **red flag...**

...a *LOT* of red flags!

Good thing, too, or I could've fallen into this gaping hole in the floor!
GASP!

A ROCKET BASEMENT!
I'd say this explains a lot, but it really doesn't!

How did Hookline and Slinker even know about this place?

sSSSSSss
!

Hookline and Slinker! I mean, uh, HOWDY, BOSS...? I'm just on my union-mandated construction worker break. I certainly wasn't *spying*.
Now, um, I've got to—

I've got to—

I've...got...to...
Got to...

I've got...

...to go...

...go and...

Heh heh!
...repair the opera house.

This is Cici Boringstories, reporting LIVE outside the **Mother of All Waffles!** According to the *Action News Now* police scanner, the chicken and waffle who escaped the Science Factory are *INSIDE* the restaurant!

MAW

This could be a **hostage situation!**

Well, I don't know about hashtags, but I **do** know about hash **browns!** They're *delicious*, and the MAW's got 'em for a dollar ninety-nine!

WHOA, little doggie!
OSED

Hookline and Slinker! I have wrangled up a scientist!

Say hello to your new lab, Dr. Doodlydoo!

New lab?
EGGSactly!
hop

You're going to invent a device that will make me BIGGER than a medium waffle!

Well? Can you make something outta all this science, Doctor? Or are you just chicken?
glance
Sciency Parts

I'm not scared, bruh. But why should I help a small waffle who rode me 'round town like a rodeo clown?

I'm a **MEDIUM** waffle! And I'll tell you why! Or, actually...

...THEY will!

Must...invent...
...**embiggen**...device...
rummage

HA HA HA! I've just about got a roof over my head...
...and a chicken scientist is inventing an embiggener for me!

Everything's coming up CRACKERDILE!
I mean, **WAFFLEDILE!**

Now all I need are more recruits for **T.A.I.L.Blazers!**
Hookline and Slinker!
Time to make flyers and spread them all over town to ***evildoers*** everywhere!

Chapter 15

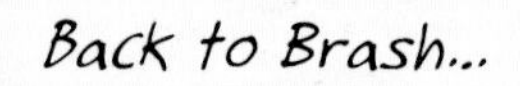
Back to Brash...

Dagnabbit!
No additional clues in the bank, *AND* I left the MAW in such a hurry I forgot to bring back the stolen money!
But of greater concern, still no sign of Mango!
$
BANK

V.E.S.T., find Mango!
Nothing? Why can't it find him?
He's not in the bank, not at the MAW... Maybe he went back to S.U.I.T. Headquarters?

Wait a minute—when we left A.R.M.S., Mango technically took *MY* V.E.S.T.!

V.E.S.T.! Find ***BRASH!***
pff

This doesn't seem good...
zzt
zzt
zzt

Uh...
zzt
zzt
zzt

AAAH!!
FOOSH

STOMP
STOMP
STOMP

GREAT.

What's this?

T.A.I.L.Blazers?
Feeling neglected in the workplace?
Want to be evil and do crimes?
Join T.A.I.L.Blazers!
Blaze a trail to success with the Total Annihilation of Idiot Law-doers!
Come to the NEW old opera house for more details. BYOS*
*Bring Your Own Snacks

BANK
HOOKLINE and SLINKER?!

Since they're working with Crackerdile, then these flyers mean...

...they're *littering!*
crumple!

But more importantly, it means Crackerdile is putting together a team of **EVIL VILLAINS!** And he's using the opera house as a *not-so-secret lair!*
I still don't know where Mango went... but my mission is and will always be STOPPING CRACKERDILE! I ***have*** to stick with the mission!
BANK

EXCUSE ME! Where do you think you're going?
Er, to the bathroom...?
EMPLOYEES ONLY

That bathroom is for EMPLOYEES only.
What? I was just in here! I'M an investment banker!
ONLY

If you're an investment banker, then why are you naked?

Today's not CASUAL FRIDAY!

Uh...

LOOK! An ELEPHANT!

Um, hi...? Why is everyone staring at me? I just want some **stamps.**
Sir, this is a BANK.

HEY!
ZIP!
EMPLOYEES ONLY

Chapter 16

How much longer, Doodlydoo?
CLOSED

You've had nearly SEVEN PAGES! Do you know how long that is in *waffle time*?!
Almost...finished...

When you're done with my EMBIGGENER, maybe you can do something about these **ants**!
My mouthwatering *wafflyness* isn't helping get rid of the pesky pests!
whee!

Bloop

RESTROOM
HOUD

Lotta construction workers. Too busy to notice me...

GASP! Dr. Doodledoo is working with Crackerdile!

But...what's with his *eyes?*
The EMBIGGENER is finished. It just needs to charge up.
Wonderful!

EMBIGGENER? I've got to sneak down there...

Careful...

Drop

WHEW! Now I just need to get past that chicken...
peck
peck
peck
AAH! Flee! *FLEE!*
We're not *fleas,* we're *ants!*

Huh? **MANGO!** He's...*undercover* as a construction worker! What a relief. Smart move, partner!

Wait a minute—***HIS*** eyes are all squiggly, too!

Mango and Dr. Doodledoo are ***HYPNOTIZED!***

Their hypnosis must be because of...
SLINKER, the SNAKE!
Science says snakes being able to hypnotize their prey is a *myth*... but Mango's eyes say science is ***mythtaken!***

If I can reach him, maybe I can snap him out of it...

Or...I could go after that Embiggener...

Save my partner... or stop Crackerdile?
I—I don't know which to do!

Mango was right. This is a **no-win scenario!**

Well, I may not win... but I won't lose another partner!

Mango! Psst! Wake up, Mango!
Man. Go?

MAN...
GO.
Yes! MANGO!
Wake—?!

SQUEEZE!

Slinker! And Hookline!
HISSS
Well, well,
well...

Mango and Brash. Nice of you to drop in. You're just in time for my big moment!

And by that I mean my EMBIGGENING MOMENT!
With this EMBIGGEN DEVICE, I, Waffledile, will become the biggest evil waffle in the world!

Then I will once and for all squash you InvestiGators like the insignificant ants you are!
HEY! That's offensive to ants!

Doodlydoo! Let the embiggening... BEGIN!
flik
BZZZZZ
VWOOOM
Ooh, it tickles!
VWOOM
VWOOM
VWOOM

VWOOM
VWOOM
VWOOM

CRASH!

Dang it! I just had this roof fixed!

Wh-What happened?
MANGO!

Brash? BRASH! I was hip-mo-tized!
I know! Can you reach your V.E.S.T. buttons?

Errrgh! NO! I'm wrapped up too tight!
Ow, my eyes... What was that bright flash?
blink blink
GASP! The light from the Embiggener—THAT must have unhypnotized you all!

Dr. Doodledoo! Can you free us?
Sure thing, bruh...

BUMP

?!
Scared of me NOW, Doodlydoo? Saddle up!

SQUAWK!
Oh, fine! Go hide, you big chicken!

Well, Gators, looks like your **CLUCK** has run out! *HA HA HA!* Get it?
That's what *YOU* think!

CONSTRUCTION WORKERS! You're no longer hypnotized! Stop that **giant waffle!**

We wasn't hypnotized.
We was doin' this job for the *dough!*

And by "*dough,*" we mean *HIM!*

And ALSO for MONEY!
You tools! He was never gonna pay you!

POWER TO THE PEOPLE!
Strike! STRIKE!

Strike him as hard as you can!
OW! Stop striking me!

PAY! US! WHAT! WE'RE! WORTH!
BRANG DANG DANG

YEOWCH!!
bzzzz

HEY! OW! I gotta get outta here!
BONK
CRUNCH

Mango and Brash still have Hookline and Slinker to deal with...
I'm gonna have a night on the town!
CLOSED

Chapter 17

Crackerdile is back, and now he's a giant WAFFLEDILE! Can you believe it, Mango?
I thought I was just seeing things! Turns out I WAS seeing things, but NOW I'm believing things!

Uh... Brash? Slinker is coming to...
So is Hookline— I mean, Bill!
Wh-Who am I?

You're Bill Plungerman, Ace Plumber!
Wh-What have I done?!

What have WEEE DONE...
Don't look, Brash! Keep your eyes shut!

The snake... I can hear it in my mind...
Don't listen to it, Bill!
Unless it's saying to let us go!

Don't look at its eyes! Slinker will hypnotize you!
NO...

NOT... THIS...

...TIME!
!?
LOOP

HISSSSSSSSSSSSSSsten...
Listen to **ME**, NOW!

HISSSSSSSSSSSSSSSSSSSSSSSSSSSS...

WE'RE FREE!
I *knew* you could do it, Bill!
ZiiP
UNCOIL

I'm **Mango** and this is **Brash**, by the way. We're **InvestiGators.**
Thanks. I...I think I remember you now, from that waffle place.

I know you tried to stop me. I didn't *WANT* to rob that bank... or hypnotize anyone... or learn Photoshop just so I could design those flyers...but I couldn't control myself. It's like I was a ***puppet,*** and this snake was ***pulling the strings.***

Well, we now know that **CRACKERDILE** was the puppet master all along!
Speaking of whom, any idea where he'd go? What his plans are?

All I know is, he wants to put together a team that will rival something called S.U.I.T....
T.A.I.L.Blazers!
Tail-what?

Uh, is it safe, yo?
Doctor Doodledoo! Yes, you can come out now.

In fact, you should take Bill back with you to the Science Factory. Hopefully the Head Scientist has figured out a cure for Hookline and Slinker by now.
'Sup.
Bruh.

Thanks, **InvestiGators!**
Anytime.

Now, come on, Mango! We've got a WAFFLE to catch up to!
Ketchup? On *waffles?*

All the construction workers took off!
But what direction did **Crackerdile** take off in?
CLOSED

We'd be able to see him if it weren't for these ***tall buildings!***

Brash!
You drive!

BRASH! I see him! Head downtown!

We're comin' for you, WAFFLEDILE!
VROOM
VROOM

Chapter 18

This is Cici Boringstories with *Action News Now*, still reporting outside the MAW.
MAW

Officer! Is there an update in the situation involving the chicken and waffle who escaped the Science Factory and are reportedly holding hostages inside?
Oh, yeah!

Turns out it was these *teenagers* who were holding the **chicken** and **waffles** hostage!
We're innocent employees!

They demanded a ransom of $3.99! Or $4.99 for **white meat only!**
That wasn't ransom! Those are the **menu prices!** We **SELL** chicken and waffles!
MAW

Ransom, menu price—either way, it's **criminal!**

Criminally *crispy!* This drumstick is **DELISH!**

JOHNSON! How many times do I have to tell you, **don't eat the hostages!**

rrrumble
What the—?!
My leg!
Is it a **flood?** An **earthquake?** The **snake-armed man?**
Let's see what the *Action News Now* helicopter in the sky has to say!

Well, Cici, I haven't appeared in the book until now, so I *should* have a ***lot*** to say... But what I'm seeing has left me speechless!
NEWS
STOMP STOMP

MOTHER of ALL WAFFLES
NEWS
Heeere's JOHNNYCAKES!

Johnnycakes are made with *cornmeal!* You're just a plain waffle!

Plane? Don't you mean... ***HELICOPTER?***
NEWS
YIKES!

Come here, you! This is the perfect ***recruitment*** opportunity! ***Every*** villain will want to join my team if they see me on the news!
NEWS
WOO
WAW
WOO
Vroom
Crunch

VROOM
Huh?

So, you want to play chicken with a giant waffle, eh, Brash?

SCRUNCH
DIVE!
That was close!

WHOA!

wobble
Hmm...
BRASH! DISTRACT HIM! I'VE GOT AN IDEA!
I'M PRETTY SURE I'VE GOT HIS ATTENTION!
STOMP
STOMP

CRANK!

Swivel!!

There's nowhere you can run I won't catch you, Agent Brash!

I've got to lure Waffledile under that bucket!

U-TURN!

Ah-HA!
Told ya so!
Ugh!
nab!

NO!

Heh heh heh! This is twice in one day you're about to be *squished* by a giant waffle! *THREE* times if we count when I stepped on the truck—
BONK
What's this?
LET HIM GO, WAFFLEDILE!
Or ***WHAT***, Agent Mango? You'll pour that concrete on me and turn me into a **giant statue?**

You do that and your partner here will suffer the same fate!
SQUEEZE

He's right!

Forget about me, Mango! It's more important to stop Daryl—I mean, *Crackerdile*—I mean, *WAFFLEDILE!* For the **GREATER GOOD!**

Here, I'll make it easy for you...

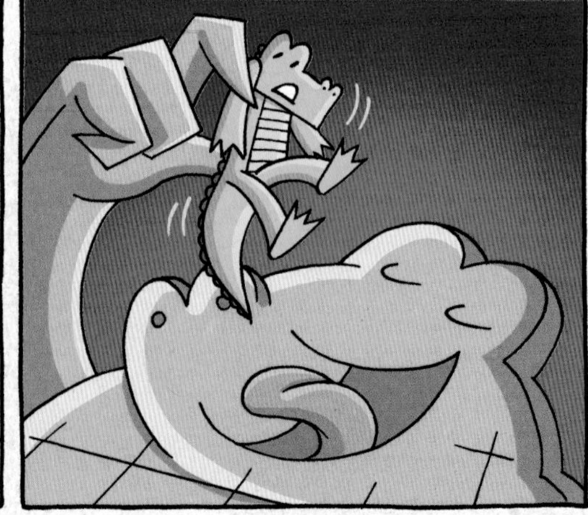

NEWS
BRASH!
Gulp

You can't dump concrete on me *AND* save your partner. But let me go, and I'll barf Brash back up!
Or, you know, he could come out the *OTHER* way...
pat
pat

Inquiring minds want to know: Do **waffles** have **butts?**

Sometimes there is no **GOOD** choice. But you still have to make **A** choice.

I'm sorry, Brash.
CRANK
YANK

For the **GREATER GOOD!**
WHAT?!
But your partner!!
Splorge

I just wanted...

...to be stronger...
than a cracker...

But not... ...like *THITH*...!
NEWS
crik
crek
Any second now, that concrete will harden! This **giant waffle** and the **InvestiGator** he swallowed will be statues ***forever!***

Suddenly!
Grapple!

It's **HOOKLINE and SLINKER!**

!
Splorp

Wha ruh—?! I feer arr **weird** inride!
Gurgle

floorp

Latch!

Shhploorrrp
Ziiipp!

*Translation: "I can't move!"

To be precise...
I'm not **just** a *news helicopter*...
but also a skilled *brain surgeon*...
Dr. Jake Hardbones!
NEWS

Tell me you got that on camera.
No, but I *did* get some pics of these **WUGGETS** for my *food blog*. No one's minding the store! #FreeWugs #Nugs4Life

Doctor! Is Brash gonna be okay?
Vital signs are weak... We need to get this gator aid at the hospital, STAT!

WOO WOO WOO WOO
SCREECH!!

Well, that's certainly convenient...?
♪

HEY! The emergency is over here!
Oh, yeah? Well there's a food emergency in my belly! And @CameraBoy64 posted that there were free wuggets!
MY FRIEND NEEDS TO GET TO THE HOSPITAL, STAT!
AND I DON'T EVEN KNOW WHAT "STAT" MEANS!
Okay, okay!
Hang in there, Brash!
Let's go!
Just so ya know, somebody owes me some wuggets.

MOTHER of ALL WAFFLES
MAW
WOO WOO WOO WOO

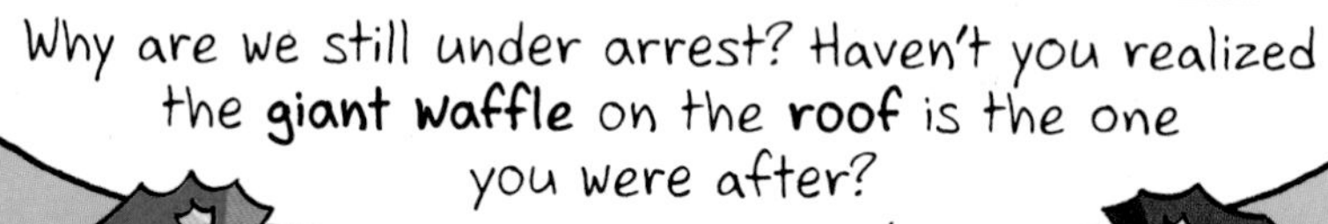
Why are we still under arrest? Haven't you realized the **giant waffle** on the **roof** is the one you were after?

He's the one that stole that money and kidnapped the chicken! Even us teenagers figured *that* out!

Well, I *guess* that makes sense...

But I hope you kids learned your lesson!

un-cuff

You heard it here first, viewers! The **snake-armed man** turned out to be a good guy, the **stolen bank money** has been recovered, the **waffle** has turned to stone, and the **chicken** has, presumably, been eaten!
Hold on... Correction: Only the chicken that was on the ***MENU*** has been eaten, ***NOT*** the one from the Science Factory. For *Action News Now*, this is Cici Boringstories, signing off.

AAAAAAND...we're out.

You didn't say anything about our **news copter** transforming into a **brain surgeon**.

Oh, *please*. No one's going to believe ***THAT.***
It sounds like something straight out of a comic book!

Chapter 19

Soon...
HOSPITAL

SNAX
pace
pace
pace

Mango?
You can come see him now.

BRASH!

Brash?
Brash, it's *me*, Mango.
Brash?

Dr. Hardbones, what's wrong with him?
As far as I can tell, *nothing!* Except he won't wake up.

Brash is in perfect health, but there must be something in his **mind** blocking him from **regaining consciousness.**

But fear not! I, **Dr. Jake Hardbones, Brain Surgeon,** will do *everything* in my power to cure Brash's *cranial condition.*
In fact, I've even called in for backup!

The **Head Scientist** from the Science Factory!
Hey-o!

If you'll recall, way back on page 57, I had the idea to invent a device that can **harness the consciousnesses** of the plumber and the snake, to aid in the separation of their bodies.
I was goofing off with the chicken, but I'll take your word for it.

I am positive that if Dr. Hardbones and I put our minds together, we can use that technology to get Brash to wake up.
Just don't *ACTUALLY* put your minds together, because that's how this mess started in the first place!

Well, it sounds like Brash's brain is in good hands.
Indeed, it is! And I should know.

My brain has LITERALLY been in this man's hands. And I feel smarter than ever!
Aw, shucks!
Thank you, doctors.
BOOP
Take care, Brash.
I'll see you soon.

Mango...
Hookline and Slinker!
I mean—**Bill Plungerman...**
Sorry.

No, that's okay. Is Brash... all right?
He's—He will be. Thank you for pulling him out of the belly of that big, bad, breakfasty beast.

Well, thanks to the **InvestiGators**, I'm no longer under that waffle's ***OR*** Slinker's control. And now I know how to snap out of the hypnosis, so I'll be able to keep from losing my head again.
There you are! So *THIS* is where everyone went!
HUFF
HUFF
Dr. Doodledoo! Did you get lost?

This dude took off into the air when we were on our way to the Science Factory! It took me this long to catch up. I can't *fly*, you know. I'm a **chicken!**
Sorry about that. For giving you the slip, I mean. Not sorry that you're a chicken.

Plus, this arm will ***really*** come in handy when I'm unclogging drains! I am a ***plumber,*** after all.

Somehow I always knew you had it in you to be a **good guy.**
Even if the trench coat made it hard to tell.

See ya around.
shake
ziiiP

HOSPITAL

Epilogue

Inside S.U.I.T. Headquarters...
Thank you for coming in, Agent Mango.
I want to commend you on stopping **Crackerdile**—*er,* **Waffledile.**
GI MOE

Though he is *technically* still at large—**VERY** large—we at least know where he is, and he won't be going anywhere anytime soon.

Thank you, sir. But I still feel like Crackerdile **won.** What he—**I**—did to Brash...
Don't be too hard on yourself, Mango. You were faced with a tough decision, and you made the right call.

And while Brash is recovering, *YOU* are now S.U.I.T.'s **top agent.** There's a lot of crime out there that needs investigating.
TOP AGENT? I dunno, sir—

You won't be in the field alone, Mango. For the time being, you'll be paired up with a *NEW* partner... Just until Brash is back on his feet.
New... partner?

I'm *proud* of you, Agent Mango. Brash would be, too. Now go out there and **keep up the good work!**
Uh, YES, SIR!

SPECTOR
C-ORB! Are you my new partner?

No. **EYE** wish! *Ha ha!*

Sven! Monocle! Eight and **Nine! Bongo** and/or **Marsha!**
Are one of *you* my new partner?
GENE

Am I late? I was told Mango is getting a new partner.
CILANTRO!

You must be my new partner!
REALLY?!
No, Mango. It's ME.

That sounds... like BRASH!!

You can call me... ROBOBRASH!
!

Even though Dr. Hardbones is still figuring out a way to wake up Brash, the Head Scientist was able to send me **downloads** of most of Brash's *personality* and *experiences*.

Then I uploaded them into this **robotic copy** I made out of spare parts.

No one's given up on the *real* Brash, Mango. RoboBrash is not a replacement for him.

But for now, out of ***all*** the other agents in S.U.I.T., no one would make a better partner for you than ***RoboBrash!***
MONOCLE made the partner, technically.

So I'm...***not*** his new partner...?

How about that, eh, Cilantro?

...Cilantro?

Hmm... You say this robot has Brash's experiences and personality? How can you tell?
Well, ask him something.
Okay... RoboBrash, what is our primary mission?
To serve the GREATER GOOD!
Don't you mean... the GATOR GOOD?
WHAT?! No, I do not! GREATER GOOD is the correct answer!

You should know this, Mango! Perhaps you need to run the **training simulation** again. *PRACTICE MAKES PERFECT!*
Yup, that sounds ***just*** like Brash!
LET'S GO!
Hurry up, Mango! WALK THIS WAY!
You mean walk like ***this?***
WHAT? *NO!* Do not walk *LIKE* me.
But you said "walk this way."
YOU KNOW WHAT I MEANT!

Later, downtown...
flap
flap
Feeling neglected in the workplace?
Want to be evil and do crimes?
Join T.A.I.L.Blazers!
Blaze a trail to success with
Come to the NEW old opera house for more details. BYOS*
*Bring Your Own Snacks
fwooooo...
FWAP!

What's this?
"Blaze a trail to success..."
Hmm...
Feeling neglected in the workplace? Want to be evil and do crimes?
Join T.A.I.L.Blazers!
Blaze a trail to success with the Total Annihilation of Idiot Law-doers!
Come to the NEW old opera house for more details. BYOS*
Snacks
This could be big...
VERY big...
THE END...?

INVESTIGATORS

How to draw **WAFFLEDILE**

1. Start with a tall oval for his body. It doesn't have to be perfect!

2. Add some big curves for his forehead, with some smaller loops for his snout. Then erase the line where his head overlaps his body (shown in blue).

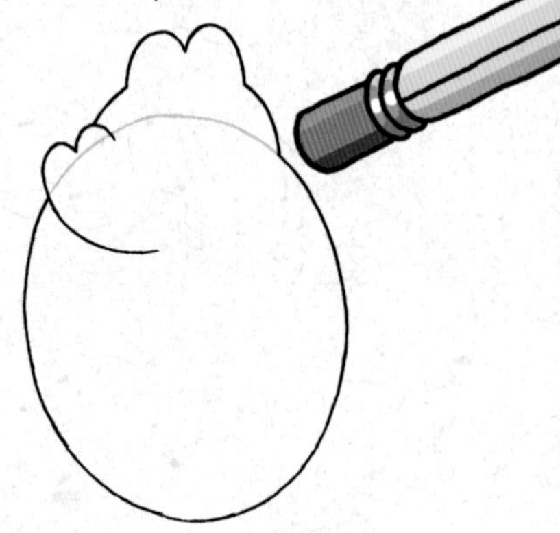

3. Draw arms with little triangles for fingers. Waffledile normally has three, but when he makes a fist you'll also see his thumb.

4. Next, add legs, with more triangles for toes. Include lines to show where his feet bend at the ankle.

5. Add details like eyes, nostrils, a mouth with pointy teeth, and a grid for a waffle pattern.

6. Draw lines around one side of his nose, head, body, arms, and legs. This will make him look 3D but also flat! Erase a tiny bit of the lines where his arms and legs connect to his body.

7. Finally, color him in. And give him some angry eyebrows, because Waffledile's always mad about something!

8. BONUS STEP! Pour maple syrup on him to turn Waffledile into a tasty treat!

New Specials!

Free Delivery!

Wac 'n' Cheese

Two of our signature waffles with baked-in macaroni and cheese centers! They're ooey, gooey, and make your tastebuds go kablooey! Served with maple sriracha.

Boneless Buffalo Wafflings

Half waffle, half wing, ALL FLAVOR! Choice of mild, medium, hot, or **volcano**. Served with celery and a smoked maple blue cheese dip. *May contain bones.*

Waldorffle Salad

A harmonious blend of apples, celery, grapes, and wafflenuts, dressed in maple mayo, and served on a bed of waffletuce.

The Chucket™

Chunks of buttermilk fried chicken served in an edible waffle-bucket! Available in small, medium, and super-double-medium.

Menu subject to change without warning

The horror! THE HORROR!

Agent Monocle is hacking into a secret database and has one last chance to crack the code. Of the numbers she's tried below, each guess has just one correct digit that's in the correct order. Knowing that, can you figure out the 3-digit passcode?

Passcode: 896 X
Passcode: 983 X
Passcode: 246 X
Passcode: 843 X
Passcode: *** ✓

C-ORB sees everything, but he can't see the connection between these nine objects. Can you tell what they have in common, and figure out if anything's missing?

Go to ***InvestiGatorsBooks.com*** *to check your answers!*

For more InvestiGREATNESS visit
InvestiGatorsBooks.com
• Case Files
• Character Bios
• Puzzles & Games
• Art Activities
• Videos
• and MORE!
Be sure to read the whole series!
COMING SOON!
InvestiGATORS
Ants in Our P.A.N.T.S.
John Patrick Green
InvestiGATORS
InvestiGATORS
Take the Plunge
Oooh! I can't wait to get my arms on that!

Invent a V.E.S.T.*!

Mango and RoboBrash! I put out the call for *new, creative, extra-special* V.E.S.T.s and our junior agents really delivered! This **SCENT DETECTOR** gadget was invented by **Clara** from **Grand Junction, Colorado.** Just provide a sample of something you want to find and it will track it by its *smell!*

*Very Exciting Spy Technology

Do you have an idea for a V.E.S.T.? Share it with us with #InvestigatorsBooks!

Special thanks to...

Aaron Polk and his flatters, Christine Brunson and Robin Fasel, for their incredible colors.
My editors, Calista Brill, Rachel Stark, and some new person, plus everyone else at First Second who's had to tolerate me.
My agent, the extraordinary Jen Linnan.
All the movies, TV shows, songs, books, etc. that I've lovingly paid homage to.
Dave Roman, Rich Zimmer, and the rest of Cryptic Press.
And of course, my brother, Bill, and the rest of my family.

John Patrick Green is a *New York Times*-bestselling author who makes books about animals with human jobs, such as *Hippopotamister*, the Kitten Construction Company series, and the InvestiGators series. John is definitely not just a bunch of animals wearing a human suit pretending to have a human job. He is also the artist and co-creator of the graphic novel series Teen Boat!, with writer Dave Roman. John lives in Brooklyn in an apartment that doesn't allow animals other than the ones living in his head.